# A vEry TOP SECRET MISSION

To LinDsay
and WeNdy
aNd to haviNg
maNy moRe
adveNtuRes!

A TEMPLAR BOOK

First published in the UK in 2015 by Templar Publishing,
part of the Bonnier Publishing Group,
Deepdene Lodge, Deepdene Avenue, Dorking, Surrey, RH5 4AT, UK
www.templarco.co.uk

Copyright © 2015 Sue Eastland

First Edition

ISBN 978-1-78370-280-0 Hardback
ISBN 978-1-78370-350-0 Paperback

Edited by Zanna Davidson
Designed by Genevieve Webster

Printed in China

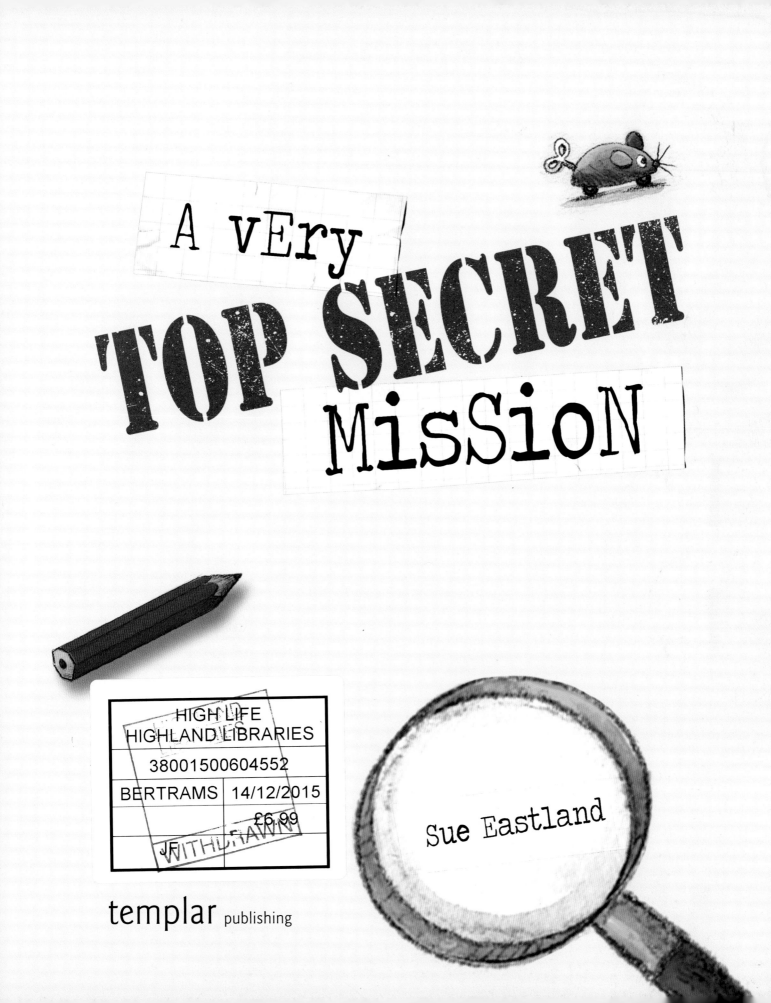

# A vEry TOP SECRET MisSioN

Sue Eastland

templar publishing

Inspector Clawso
OFFICE

It all started when a large brown envelope marked

# TOP SECRET

dropped through the letter box.

The envelope was addressed to me!

The letter was from the Head of C.O.D. (CAT'S ORGANISATION OF DETECTIVES).

I had been assigned a very TOP SECRET mission!

Dear Inspector Clawso,

Your mission is to solve the mysterious crime of Mr Ginger's stolen cat food.

Only two clues were found at the crime scene (enclosed). We need your expert help!

Yours Sincerely

Head of C.O.D.

The clues appeared to be two scraps of card cut from a packet of FISH. FINGERS.

I thought to myself,
WHO is this 'FIsH FiNgErS' character and WHY
are they stealing Mr Ginger's cat food?
There is definitely something fishy going on here and
I need some assistance. . .

## "Can YOU help me solve this crime?"

Remember, this is a very TOP SECRET mission
so I need someone very special to help me.
Do you think you have what it takes to be a SUPER SLEUTH?

## Are you...

super coOl? ☐

Super SmART? ☐

Super stEalthy? ☐

ANd do yOu like tuNa pizzA? ☐

TUNA PIZZA

Inspector Clawso
OFFICE

If you can answer YES
to SOME or ALL of the
above, come with me into
my office.

Before we go on a very **TOP SECRET** mission
it's important to make notes and plan for success.

# NoTes

The victim – Mr Ginger

First Clues

FISH

FINGERS

Dear Head of C.O.D.
I accept this
Very Top SeCret
MiSsion

ROYAL TYPE

TUNA PIZZA

CAT DETECTIVE

EXECUTIVE

TOY

A-D

E-J

K-P

Q-Z

PAW PRINTS

SECRET FILES

009

TOP SECRET

Did you know that nine tenths of SUCCESS...

...is in the PREPARATION?

The other
tenth
is pure
**GENIUS!**

Have you got
your notebook
ready?

Let's go up on
the roof to get a
**good look**
at the
neighbourhood.

C.O.D

Mr Dog's House

Mr Mouse's House

WHO can you SEE?
WHERE do they live?

Let's begin our investigations at Mr Ginger's house.

FLUMP!

BIG G

Are you ready?
Let's go in.

I'm now going to ask **Mr Ginger** a few questions. . .

Hmm. . . let's go back to my office and put together **everything** we've learnt.

We know from our SUPER POWERS of OBSERVATION that
Miss Birdy, Mr Mouse and Mr Dog all live nearby,
so let's add them to our list of **suspects**, not forgetting
we've got a mystery Scary Monster suspect too!

"Hello, Miss Birdy! We would like to ask you about the theft of Mr Ginger's cat food. Where were you at 8 o'clock supper time?"

"I was visiting Mr Mouse," chirps Miss Birdy.

"I see. And while you were in the area of the crime, did you find anything unusual?"

"Yes, this green feather. It was near the tree by Mr Ginger's house."

"How interesting! That will be all for now, thank you."

Now there's just enough time to complete a Super Sleuth Test before we pay a visit to Mr Mouse...

# SUPER SLEUTH TEST 1

## Complete your first mission to earn a gold star.

Use your SUPER COOL POWERS of DEDUCTION:
Match each owl with the correct feather.

Tread carefully. Mice can be very sensitive creatures.

SNEAK

LEAP

CRASH

"Hello, Mr Mouse. We'd like to ask you about the theft of Mr Ginger's cat food. . ."

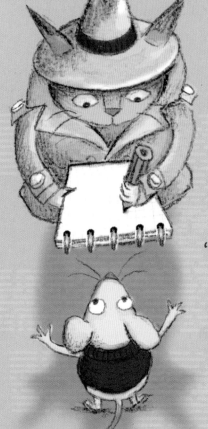

GREEN FINGERS

Where were you at 8 o'clock supper time?"

"I was at home," squeaks Mr Mouse. "Miss Birdy came to visit me and then we went out together to see Mr Dog."

"I see. Did you notice anything suspicious?"

"I found this cardboard tooth near Mr Ginger's house. It looks like one of mine but much bigger!"

Hmm. . . let's try another Super Sleuth Test before we visit our next suspect.

Time to visit Mr Dog. Hang onto your hat!
This could get dangerous. Dogs are very tricky creatures.

SWISH

CRAASH

CLOMP

"Hello, Mr Dog. Where were you at 8 o'clock supper time?"

"I was here, by the bins," barks Mr Dog. "Mis
Birdy and Mr Mouse came to visit me."

"I see. Did you find anything that you thought was strange?"

"Well, yes. I found this odd brown sock!"

"Mmm. . .
**very odd**
indeed!"

# SUPER SLEUTH TEST 3

## Complete your third mission to earn a gold star.

Use your SUPER COOL POWERS of OBSERVATION:
Spot 5 differences between these dustbins.

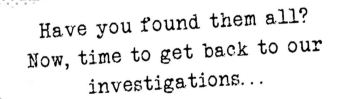

Have you found them all?
Now, time to get back to our
investigations...

There's much more to this than I thought! We can remove three suspects: Miss Birdy, Mr Mouse and Mr Dog all have alibis.
(That means they can prove they were somewhere else when the crime was committed.)

NOTES

The victim – Mr Ginger

Miss Birdy

Mr Mouse

Mr Dog

First Clues

FISH FINGERS

stolen cat food

SUSPECTS

A scary monster face with feathers like a bird, floppy brown ears like a dog, fishy little eyes and big scary mouse teeth!

New Clues

That leaves just one suspect...

...the scary monster!

TUNA PIZZA

CAT DETECTIVE

EXECUTIVE TOY

PAW PRINTS

SECRET FILES

ROYAL TYPE

A-D
E-J
K-P
Q-Z

Hmm... something still feels a bit fishy, don't you think?

We need BRAIN FOOD!
Let's have a sliCe of tuna pizza.

It's nearly 8 o'clock. . .
I think we should do a
STAKE OUT at the crime scene.

Come with me. . .

Adopt stealth mode!

**LISTEN!** What's that noise?

**QUICK!** Let's hide!

GRUFFLE-GRUFFLE

. . . sc-scary monster!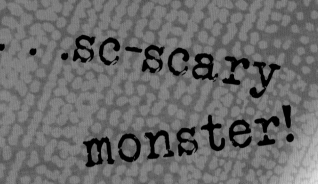

UH-OH!

Or is it?

"Well, well, well. . . Who do we have here?

It's. . .

MR Ginger!

So you've been stealing your

own cat food disguised as a

scary monster!"

"It was an impressive disguise. You used the scary monster costume to make it look like a BIRD. . . a MOUSE. . . or a DOG was involved in the crime. You nearly got away with it, BUT you dropped a few clues along the way!

A green feather

A fake front tooth

A floppy brown sock

And the reason for you stealing YOUR OWN cat food, apart from getting EXTRA SNACKS, was that you were collecting these tokens for a

## PURRFECT HOLIDAY!"

"Yes, it's all **true**," confesses Mr Ginger. "But I really am **very sorry!**"

Well it looks like we've solved this fishy crime at last.
I couldn't have accomplished this very TOP SECRET mission
without your help.

WELL DONE!

Here's your official
SUPER SLEUTH badge

and certificate...

SUPER SLEUTH

...and a slice of
tuna pizza of course!

CERTIFICATE
**Top Secret Mission Complete**

Levels Passed

☑ SUpEr CoOl

☑ SUpEr STeAlthY

☑ SUpEr SmArt

★ ★ ★

3 GOLD STAR AWARD
STATUS **PURE GENIUS**

You can download your own badge and certificate at www.templarco.co.uk/topsecretmission